Amazing Maisy's Family Tree

written by Lynn Zirkel
illustrated by Peter Bowman

MAISY didn't know you know
no never knew what we all know
that hers were fingers of the greenest
sort that anyone can grow.

She only had to touch a twig,
a twig that may appear to be
the deadest twig you ever saw,
to grow the biggest tree.

Oxford University Press
Oxford Toronto Melbourne

IT started with a single seed
in a worn-out pot on a 'nothing else to do day'.

The seed grew and the need grew in Maisy
to plant a million seeds in every pot she'd got.

So, on a day that brightened into a starry night
Maisy planted her million seeds in almost
a million pots, not quite, but quite a lot.
Before she went to bed she gazed out of her window
at the dazzling stars and wished a secret wish
on the most dazzling star of all.

The starry night fizzled into a grey dawn,
but in Maisy's bedroom spring had sprung in almost
a million pots, in almost a million colours.

The seeds had grown . . .

EVERYBODY 'Oooohed' and 'Aaahed' at Maisy's
mammoth mountain of hanging, spotted,
        evergrowing,
        gnarled and knotted,
        spiky, prickly,
        tickly,
        'flowery, stripey,
        dotted,
        pert and pretty,
        potted plants,
because the plants were very nice, but . . .

they grew bigger,

MAISY'S mum, dad, granny, and extremely grumpy grandad grim soon began to groan and gripe and whine about all the hanging vine and such. It had become by far too much. 'There isn't room for all of us,' they moaned.

And while the gruesome bunch of grizzly grumps groused and groaned, amongst the eaves a million leaves with ears rustled and agreed.

and became more cunning,

LATER in the day, much later, as the sky was
turning grey with evening, Maisy's gran, a gran
much older than the oldest hill, sat on the old
porch chair to knit a scarf.

The scarf she knitted was green, and as her needles
clicked, her knitting grew as long as the silent
shadows surrounding the porch. But the silence
of the shadows was soon disturbed by a rustling as . .

something dark and green emerged,
green and dark they say it came,
and wrapped itself round Maisy's gran
from head to toe and back again.

very long and very green . . .

Now being a rather prune-like gran,
she wasn't missed by Maisy in the least.

Maisy was far more taken with her budding
shrubs than ever she had been with her groaning
gran, and took to cutting bits off all the best
ones.

One bit in particular grew and
                    grew and
                    grew until it was as fat
as mum and as thick as winter fog, and Maisy
clipped from it a pair of pets,
a cat called Kin and Bark the dog.

and they ran wild and free.

Now Maisy's grandad was a mean and miserly
grim and grumpy
pinched and poky
grandad if ever there was one.

He didn't like Kin and Bark and so he formed
a dark and horrid plan, the horrid man.

But sadly, deadly dark and beastly horrid plans
go wrong.

They wound around things,

GRUMPY grandad grim's plan went very
wrong indeed, for, as he picked up speed
hurtling after Kin and Bark, he sailed over
the bannisters in a very splendid arc . . .
      flip flop,
      flip flop plop, he landed
in a heap of peat and disappeared completely
except for his feet, which were very big feet
for such an average-sized grandad.

spilling down things.

Summer came and everywhere
was overrun with summer blooms
that sent their sunny fragrance
overflowering into all the rooms.

With the summertime and sunshine and the watering
they got, the plants grew wild and woolly. Soon,
everything that should never grow if watered
every day for a hundred years grew
                    and grew
                and grew
            and grew.

They bloomed in great bunches.

MAISY'S mum didn't like the way things were
growing bigger every day. Nor did she like the way
her family was growing smaller every day.

'I must be careful of these bloomin' plants,' she
   thought.
But even as she thought the thought, something green
crept up and gave her . . .

        just a gentle little push,
        a tiny shove was all she got
        and Maisy's mum became the subtle
        added flavour in the pot of tea she was making.

Bees buzzed around them,

OF all the gruesome grizzly grumps, Maisy's dad was the only one left.

But instead of being lonely, he found he liked the peace and quiet to sit and smoke his pipe in peace. Poor dad, he didn't know that he would be the next to go, but he was, because . . .

insects lived on them,

A rare experimental herb
had taken root inside the pipe
that Maisy's dad, quite unaware
had settled down to huff
                    and
                    puff
and smoke in peace that night.

One puff was all it took to make poor dad
as dizzy as a top and send him spinning
off to bed. And though tucked in and safe,
he watched in dismay as a cactus puffed itself
to such a size before his startled eyes
until, where once had lain dizzy dad in his
room, there sat a cactus as fat as a BIG
green balloon.

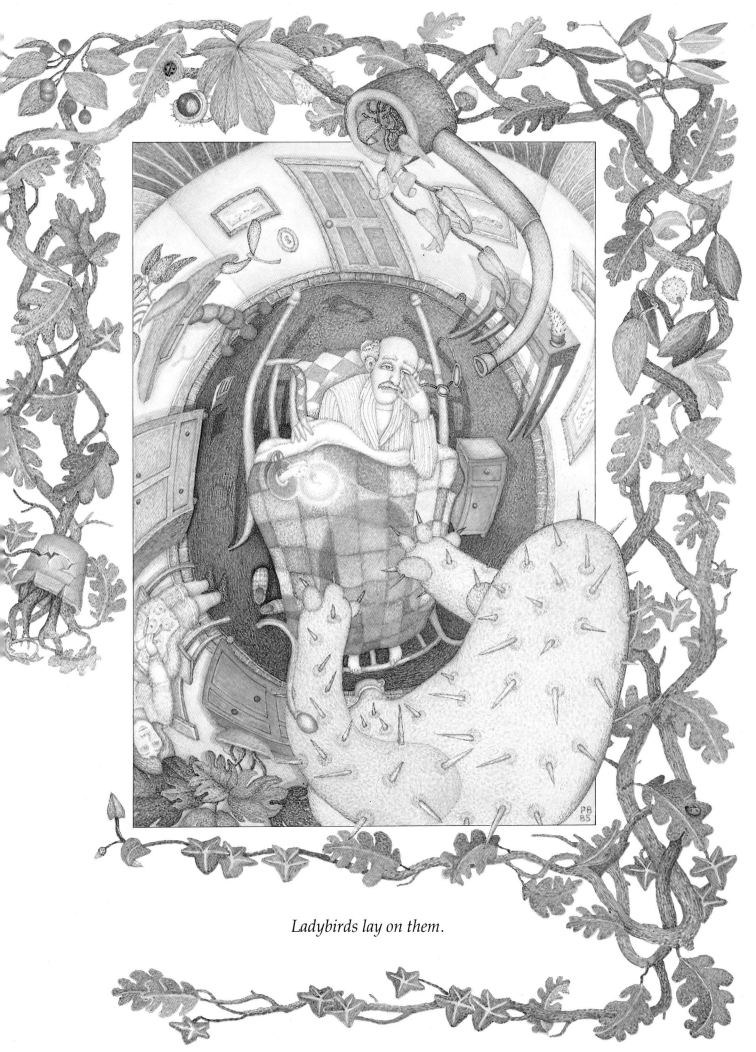

Ladybirds lay on them.

SUMMER mellowed, slowly mellowed
into autumn's golden brown
and though the flowers of summer faded
nothing slowed the growing down.

Maisy was as happy as a bee on a flower and saw
that with the autumn came the vegetables and fruit
that grew as big as dinosaurs.

With their giant size she found at every country
show she walked away with every prize.

And who knows what hid in them?

Aₗₗ the local papers wrote stories about her,
but still her fame didn't spread as quickly
as the plants inside her house.

Soon the house itself began to sprout, and with
each passing day she saw it growing in a very
tree-like way.

Then Maisy stood in awe of what she'd done,
for surely in all the houses
            in every city,
            there wasn't one
            as strange or pretty.
            No house as green,
            as brown, as strong,
            no house with branches
            quite as long,
no house that grew with such alarming speed
as this, that started with a single seed.

Or what mysteries they held?

THE wind of winter whistles cold
and with each frozen breath it breathes
a soft and silent song of snow
that settles over autumn leaves.

The snow smothered them,

FOR spring had sprung and summer blossomed,
winter walked in autumn's wake,
but underneath their coloured coats
the seasons had conspired to make . . .

AMAZING MAISY'S FAMILY TREE

A tree so BIG
A tree so T
        A
        L
        L

A tree so high it brushed the clouds
that sailed the sky.

A family tree that truly couldn't fall.

until again the spring uncovered them,
and all their glorious secrets.

AND perhaps the family that one
                              by one
                              by one
                              by one, disappeared,
                                    aren't really gone.

For maybe Maisy's plants are kinder
than I've made them out to be, and if you look
beside things and behind things,
you will find things. A clue or two or three
or even four things, maybe more things, that
will point to Maisy's family.

And maybe they are better people having had a
horrid fright. And maybe that's the wish that
Maisy wished upon a star that night.

Oxford University Press, Walton Street, Oxford OX2 6DP

© Lynn Zirkel 1986

Illustrations © Peter Bowman 1986

First published 1986

British Library Cataloguing in Publication Data
Bowman, Peter
Amazing Maisy's family tree.
I. Title   II. Zirkel, Lynn
823'.914[J.]   P27
ISBN 0–19–279830–8

Set by Oxford Publishing Services, Oxford
Printed in Hong Kong